# Contents

To Heidi and friends

# Zack Black

## and the

# Ink Trick!

Scripture Union, 207–209 Queensway, Bletchley, Milton Keynes, MK2 2EB,
United Kingdom
Email: info@scriptureunion.org.uk
Website: www.scriptureunion.org.uk

Scripture Union Australia, Locked Bag 2, Central Coast Business Centre,
NSW 2252, Australia
Website: www.scriptureunion.org.au

Scripture Union USA, PO Box 987, Valley Forge, PA 19482, USA
Website: www.scriptureunion.org

British Library Cataloguing-in-Data
A catalogue record of this book is available from the British Library.

Printed and bound in Great Britain by Creative Print and Design (Wales),
Ebbw Vale

Cover and internal illustration by Jane Eccles
Cover design by PRE Design
Internal design and layout by Richard Jefferson

Scripture Union is an international Christian charity working with
churches in more than 130 countries, providing resources to bring the
good news of Jesus Christ to children, young people and families and to
encourage them to develop spiritually through the Bible and prayer.

As well as our network of volunteers, staff and associates who run holidays,
church-based events and school Christian groups, we produce a wide range
of publications and support those who use our resources through training
programmes.

# Chapter 1

# "Boys keep out!"

Zack Black liked invisible ink.
Not fizzy drink. Or a big stink.
And he hated pink...

Thump! The football banged against his sister's window.

Two cross faces appeared. It was the girls.

Zack and Alex looked at one another and laughed.

"Silly girls," said Zack. "What do they do in their room all day?"

"Must be hiding something!" said Alex. "And we – the spies – are going to find out what it is! Come on!"

Alex and Beth had come to stay for the weekend. Alex was in Zack's class at school. Beth was in the same class as Megan, Zack's big sister.

It was fun having them to stay, but Beth annoyed Zack. She and Megan had already put a big sign on their door, saying: "Boys keep out!"

Alex had a new spy kit.

"Look at this, Zack!" said Alex. "This is my spy pen! It can record voices! Look, you press this button and speak: "ZACK ZACK ZACK!" Then you play it back... Listen!"

DACK DACK DACK!

"Cool, isn't it?"
Zack wanted one too.

"When the girls are downstairs, we'll put the pen in Megan's room and press Record!" said Alex. "They will come back and start talking, and later we can listen to what they say! Clever, eh?"

Zack didn't really *want* to know. It would just be about make-up and glitter. Yuck.

"We need to find out what they are doing!" said Alex. "They might be planning an attack!"

"Not very likely!" thought Zack. But he liked the idea of being spies.

"OK, let's do it," said Zack.

Later, when the girls were watching television, Zack and Alex crept into Megan's room. They left the spy pen on the windowsill.

"Look, Zack!" said Alex. "It's Beth's diary!"

He held up a pink fluffy book, with TOP SECRET written on the front.

"This will be funny!" said Alex, and he opened the book.

Alex laughed out loud. "Look! Beth says—"

But just at that moment, Beth and Megan burst into the room!

Alex threw the book at Zack.
Zack caught it.

Beth snatched the diary from
Zack. "Don't read my diary!"

"But I didn't!" said Zack.

Megan looked cross too. "I'm
going to tell Mum!" she said in
a bossy voice.

# Trick sweets

Before Megan had time to find Mum, there came a shout from Zack's room.

"Zack! What have you done to your bed? Look!"

Mum was pointing at Zack's bed. There was a big black ink mark on it.

"You must have left a pen there, and it has leaked everywhere," said Mum. "This ink won't wash out!"

"And Zack read Beth's diary!" said Megan.

"Leave the girls alone, please," said Mum crossly. "You can do some jobs, if you have nothing else to do. Get Dodger a drink."

Zack was fed up. He hadn't left a pen on his bed. And he hadn't read Beth's diary. Why was everyone blaming him?

Then Alex had another bright idea. He took some small red sweets out of his pocket.

"Let's put some trick sweets in your room. We'll know if the girls sneak into your room and eat them, because they'll have a nasty surprise! They're really made of pepper!"

Alex put a few trick sweets on Zack's table.

"Right, let's go downstairs," he whispered to Zack. "When the girls leave their room, we can get our spy pen back, too. Let's hope they find the sweets!"

Zack and Alex could hear the girls chatting in Megan's room.

"Let's go outside," said Alex in a loud voice, so the girls could hear. "We'll save these sweets for later!"

The boys went downstairs loudly, but hid round the corner of the stairs to keep watch.

"Hey, Megan!" said Beth. "The boys have left some sweets in their room! Come on!"

"Watch out, Dodger!" said Megan, as the dog raced past them into Zack's room. "Looks like he's found the sweets too!"

Dodger jumped on the table and started munching a sweet. Beth popped one into her mouth too.

URRRGH!

She quickly spat the sweet out. Dodger coughed and sneezed.

"These are trick sweets!" said Beth, coughing too. She tripped and landed on Zack's model spaceship. "Ow!"

# Chapter 3

# Invisible ink

Zack and Alex crept back upstairs and got the spy pen from Megan's room.

Then they tried to sneak past Zack's room, but it was too late. The girls knew they had been tricked, and were very angry.

19

"You poisoned me!" shouted Beth.

"Well, you've smashed up my spaceship!" said Zack.

Beth was still coughing and spluttering. So was Dodger.

"Poor Dodger!" said Megan.

"What's wrong with Dodger?" said Mum, hearing all the noise.

"Zack poisoned us!" said Beth, pulling a funny face.

Mum frowned and looked tired. "Lunch will be ready in ten minutes. Please try to get on with each other until then!"

The girls went downstairs to get Beth and Dodger a drink of water from the sink tap.

Great trick, wasn't it?

Zack wasn't so sure. He hoped Dodger wouldn't be sick.

"Now, let's listen to the spy pen!" said Alex. He pressed a button.

There was a fuzzy noise. Then it got a bit clearer. Zack could just make out Beth's voice.

"My sister is really silly sometimes," said Alex, trying to cheer Zack up. "But don't worry. Look! I've got an invisible ink pen. You can write Beth a letter in invisible ink!"

Alex handed Zack the pen. "Write something rude!" said Alex. Zack tried to think of something clever. He wanted to make Alex laugh.

Zack wrote: "Beth stinks!" on a piece of paper. Then he added: "Beth tells lies."

The writing was invisible.

"You can only read it with my special spy torch!" Alex said.

He shone the torch on the paper. Suddenly, Zack could read his wobbly writing.

Alex posted the letter under Megan's door.

Zack was glad that Beth didn't have a spy torch. She couldn't read what he had written, could she?

# Chapter 4

# The spy kit

At lunchtime, Zack thought about Alex's spy kit. Although Zack wasn't sure it was a good idea to play tricks on Beth, he thought the spy kit was really cool. He wanted one, but Alex said it cost five pounds!

Zack had been saving up his pocket money. He had three pounds and 41 pence. Not enough for the spy kit yet...

Then, after lunch, Zack saw Dad's wallet on the kitchen table. It was bulging with coins. Would Dad notice if Zack took some?

Zack checked that no one was looking. He opened Dad's wallet. His heart was thumping. Zack felt a bit funny.

10p, 20p, 50p, another 50p, 5p... Zack counted the money. He held it in his sticky hand.

He quickly put the wallet back where he had found it.

Dad came into the kitchen.

Hey Zack!

"Do you and Alex want to come to town with me this afternoon?" said Dad. "You could bring your pocket money."

Zack didn't look at his dad. He felt bad about taking the money. But he *did* want the spy kit.

"Yes, Dad!" he said. "Can we go to All-Toys?"

"Come on, then," said Dad. "Let's go!"

A couple of hours later, Dad and the boys came back home. Megan and Beth were watching cartoons in the lounge. They looked up when Zack ran in, smiling.

Megan saw an All-Toys bag in Zack's hand.

"I got a spy kit, just like Alex's!" said Zack. "There's a pen with invisible ink, and a torch that shows up the writing!"

"Hey, I got an invisible letter today," said Megan. "Can we try it on that?"

Before Zack could say anything, Megan had grabbed the torch and rushed off to find the letter that Alex had posted under Megan's door.

She came back, shining the torch on the writing.

"Look!" she said. "It says... Oh!"

Zack felt really silly as Megan read: "Beth stinks! Beth tells lies."

Beth ran out of the room, looking upset.

"Zack!" said Dad. "That's not very kind, is it? Think about it."

"But she does tell lies, Dad," said Zack. "She got ink on my

bed and then said it was me. And she said I read her diary, but I didn't. And she broke my spaceship."

"Try to forgive her," said Dad. "She's having a hard time at the moment."

"But she's always shutting us out of the room and saying rude things to us. I'm fed up of it."

Dad looked sad. "I know it's not easy, but remember that it's important to forgive her. Not just once, but again and again. God forgives *us* over and over again when we do things wrong."

"Zack," said Megan, suddenly. "Where did you get five pounds from to buy the spy kit?"

Zack felt his face turning red. "Well, I've saved it up. And the Tooth Fairy gave me some," he mumbled.

"That was weeks ago. You spent that money on comics!" said Megan.

Zack didn't want to tell lies to Dad.

"I'm really sorry, Dad," he said quietly.

Zack looked down at his feet. Dad was quiet for a moment.

"Zack, it was wrong of you to take my money. But thank you for telling me," he said.

Zack felt much better now that he had told Dad the truth.

Zack and Alex ran upstairs with the new spy kit. On the carpet in Zack's room there was a massive pink blob.

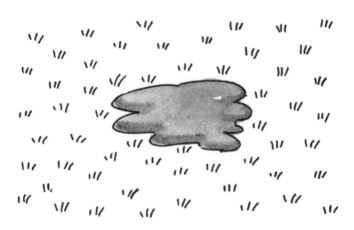

"Look at that!" said Alex. "You're going to be in trouble again!"

"But I didn't do it!" said Zack. "I bet it was the girls."

"Let's look in their room," said Alex.

Alex and Zack crept into Megan's room to look around.

Zack saw a bottle of nail varnish. It was the same colour as the blob on his carpet.

"Right!" said Zack. Zack picked up a pen. He picked up Beth's diary. He scribbled all over it!

Beth and Megan appeared at the door.

"What are you doing?" shouted Beth.

"I'm telling Mum!" said
Megan.

"I don't care!" said Zack, and
he ran past the girls.

Beth pushed Zack. Zack
tripped over Dodger, who had
come to see what all the fun
was about.

Zack fell over Dodger with a
big crash.

"Arrgh! My ankle!" he
groaned.

# Chapter 5

# The spies

The rest of the day was no fun for Zack.

His ankle really hurt. Dad took him to hospital to have an X-ray. They had to wait three long hours at the hospital.

Zack's ankle was wrapped in a big bandage.

"It's not broken," Dad told Mum when they got home at last.

"But Zack must rest his leg for two weeks. No football, and no running around the house."

This was bad news.

Beth looked worried when she saw Zack that evening.

But Zack was still cross with Beth. He didn't want to talk to her. It was her fault that he was hurt. It was her fault that he couldn't play football.

"Leave me alone!" he said quietly.

"Zack!" said Mum. "Beth's trying to be friendly. Don't be rude, please."

"Well, it's all her fault," said Zack. "She pushed me."

"I'm really sorry, Zack," said Beth.

But Zack didn't want to listen.

"I just want to go to bed," said Zack. He had been waiting all evening for a jam sandwich, but now he wasn't hungry.

Mum helped Zack get ready
for bed.

"What's going on, Zack?"
asked Mum. "Why won't you
forgive Beth?"

Zack took a deep breath.

"She's been getting me into
trouble. She put ink on my bed
and nail varnish on my carpet."

"But you've been playing tricks on her too, I think," said Mum.

"Anyway, how would you feel if Dad or I didn't forgive you when you said sorry? Like for taking Dad's money without asking?" asked Mum.

"Oh no!" thought Zack.

"Dad must have told Mum about that!"

"God tells us to forgive each other," Mum went on, "just like he forgives us, over and over again. When Dad or I see you all squabbling, we feel sad.

We love you and want you to get on with each other. God sees us hurting other people, and it makes him sad too. But if we say sorry, then he forgives us."

Zack thought about that for a while. "Maybe I'm the one who should say sorry," he said quietly.

He suddenly felt a bit better. His leg still hurt, but he knew that in the morning he would sort things out with Beth.

On Sunday morning, Dodger came bounding into the room.

"Watch it, Dodger!" shouted Zack. "My leg!"

But Dodger didn't care about his leg. He licked Zack's face.

Zack tried to sit up.

"Hey look!" said Alex, wriggling out of his sleeping bag. "There's a note under the door!"

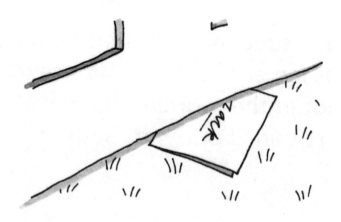

Zack opened the note. It was from Beth.

Dear Zack,

Sorry. Can we be friends?

From Beth.

Alex opened the door. Outside, there was a parcel.

"Open it, then!" said Alex. "What is it?"

Zack opened the parcel and found a packet of jammy dodgers.

Beth and Megan peered round the door.

"Friends?" asked Beth.

"Spies!" said Zack, smiling. "You need to say the secret password!"

"Let me guess," said Megan. "Ink?"

"You got it!" said Zack.